Billie B Brown

www.BillieBBrown.com

The Secret Message
published in 2011 by
Hardie Grant Egmont
85 High Street
Prahran, Victoria 3181, Australia
www.hardiegrantegmont.com.au

A CiP record for this title is available from the National Library of Australia

Text copyright © 2011 Sally Rippin
Illustration copyright © 2011 Aki Fukuoka
Logo and design copyright © 2011 Hardie Grant Egmont

Design and typeset by Stephanie Spartels

Printed in Australia by McPherson's Printing Group

1 3 5 7 9 10 8 6 4 2

Billie B Brown

The Secret Message

By Sally Rippin

Illustrated by Aki Fukuoka

hardie grant EGMONT

Chapter One

Billie B Brown has one pair of bathers, seven seashells and a bucket and spade. Do you know what the B in Billie B Brown stands for?

Beach!

It is the summer holidays and Billie B Brown is at the beach.

Today Billie is going to make a sandcastle. She is going to make the biggest, most beautiful sandcastle you have ever seen.

Seven seashells

A bucket and spade

One pair
of bathers

3

Billie's mum reads a book under a beach umbrella. Her dad reads the newspaper. Sometimes they even fall asleep. Can you imagine? They are absolutely no fun at all!

Billie puts on some sunscreen and sits out in the sun.

She starts to build a sandcastle. There's a family with two girls nearby. The girls are building a sandcastle too. Their sandcastle is very big and very beautiful.

Billie feels a teensy bit **jealous**. She wishes her best friend Jack was here to help her.

'Lunch!' Billie's mum calls.

Just in time. Billie's tummy

is growling like a tiger!

Billie trudges up the beach to sit in the shade. Billie's mum gives her a sandwich. Even though Billie has wiped her hands, her banana sandwich still tastes **crunchy**.

Billie's dad says, 'Would you like extra sand in your witch?'

He says that every time
they eat lunch
at the beach,
but Billie
still laughs.

Billie watches
the other girls make
their castle. One of them
looks about the same
age as Billie.

She has ginger hair and freckles and she is wearing pink and white polka-dot bathers. Billie wishes *she* had fancy bathers.

'Why don't you ask if you can play with them?' Billie's mum says.

Billie shakes her head. She feels shy.

She would love to play with those kids, but she is too **scared** to go over and ask them.

What if they don't want to play with me? Billie thinks.

What if they laugh at me or they are mean?

No, Billie decides. *It is much safer just to play on my own.*

Chapter Two

Billie finishes her
sandwich and goes
back to her sandcastle.
She decides that it needs
a moat. Billie digs and
digs and digs.

Her spade hits something hard. **Clink!** Billie reaches into the hole. She feels something smooth.

Billie digs deeper and pulls out a tiny bottle. It is as green as the sea and as small as her hand.

Billie holds the bottle up to the sun.

The glass is so dark that it is impossible to see what's inside.

A girl walks past collecting shells. She sees the bottle in Billie's hand.

'Ooh!' she says.
'What's inside?'

Billie shrugs. 'I don't know,' she says.

'It's beautiful,'
says the little girl.
She reaches out her
sandy fingers to touch
the green glass.

'I'm Billie,' says Billie.

'I'm Charlotte,' the
little girl says. 'That's my
sister, Harriet.' She points
to the girl in the fancy
bathers.

Harriet, Billie thinks.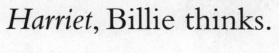

That's a nice name.

Then she has an idea.

A super-dooper idea.

'Actually, I think
there's a secret message
inside the bottle,'
Billie whispers to
Charlotte. 'It's probably
from a pirate.'

'Wow!' says Charlotte.
Her eyes open wide.
'I have to tell Harriet!
She loves pirates!'

Billie watches Charlotte
run along the beach to
where Harriet is waiting.

Chapter Three

That afternoon, Billie
and her mum and dad
walk to the shops to buy
ice-creams. Billie always
chooses banana choc-chip
with sprinkles.

Billie has to eat her
ice-cream very quickly
so that it doesn't melt.
Already it is drip-drip-
dripping on her toes.

Billie walks back to the beach and finishes her ice-cream. When she looks up, there is a girl standing in front of her. It's Harriet. Billie's heart begins to flap about like a butterfly.

'My sister told me you found a bottle with a message inside,' says Harriet. 'Can I see?'

Billie pulls the bottle out of her pocket.

Harriet squints at the dark glass. 'I can't see any message inside,' she frowns.

'It has to be very small,' Billie says. 'To fit in the bottle.'

'Hmm,' Harriet says. 'Who do you think wrote it?'

Billie shrugs. She feels a
little bit **shy**. 'Probably
a pirate.'

Harriet smiles. 'Or maybe
a *princess*?' she says.
'Captured by pirates?'

'Or maybe the prince
trying to save her?' says
Billie excitedly. 'But his
boat has sunk and now he's
stuck on a desert island!'

'Yeah!' Harriet says.
'Hey, do you want to come and help us build our sandcastle?'

Billie looks at her mum and dad.

'Sure!' says Billie's dad.

'Let me put some more sunscreen on you first,' says Billie's mum.

Billie wiggles as her mum covers her in sunscreen. Then she runs after Harriet to the big, beautiful sandcastle. Charlotte is waiting for them there.

Billie holds the little bottle in her hands. The girls all try to guess what's inside.

Billie feels very special
to have found such a
magical thing.

Then Billie has an idea.
Carefully she balances
the little green bottle on
top of the sandcastle.
It looks magnificent!
Now it is the biggest,
most beautiful sandcastle
on the beach.

Charlotte jumps up and
down excitedly. Harriet
does a handstand.
Billie decides she will do
a handstand too.

But she is not used to doing handstands on the soft sand. She wibbles and wobbles, then…
crash! Billie falls down. Right on top of the big, beautiful sandcastle!

Harriet and Charlotte gasp.

Billie stands up quickly. But it is too late. The sandcastle is ruined.

Billie stares at the crushed
sandcastle. Right in the
middle is her little green
bottle. It has cracked
neatly in half. The girls
kneel down to look at it.

And that's when they see…there is nothing inside it. Nothing at all.

Billie covers her face with her hands. Big fat tears roll down her cheeks. She grabs the two pieces of the bottle and runs back to her mum and dad.

Chapter Four

Billie has decided that
this is the worst day ever.
She has made a sandcastle
and broken a sandcastle.
She has found a bottle and
broken a bottle.

Worst of all, she made
a friend but now she is
sure the friendship will
be broken.

Harriet knows there
wasn't any message
in the bottle. Billie was
just making up stories.
Harriet will never
want to be friends with
Billie now!

Billie sits on her towel
under the beach umbrella
and cries.

'Why don't you just
say sorry?' Billie's mum
suggests.

Billie shakes her head.
She is much too **scared**
to go and talk to those
girls now. Especially after
everything she has done!

Billie B Brown is
good at lots of things.
She is good at the
monkey bars and she is
good at making cubbies.

She is good at soccer
and she is good at
midnight feasts. But the
thing that Billie B Brown
is best at is coming up
with good ideas.

Billie wipes her eyes.
She looks at the little
broken bottle in her hand.
And then she has an idea.

It is the superest-dooperest
idea she has had all day!

Can you guess what
Billie is thinking?

Billie tears off a corner
of her dad's newspaper.
Then she takes his pencil
and writes in very small
writing.

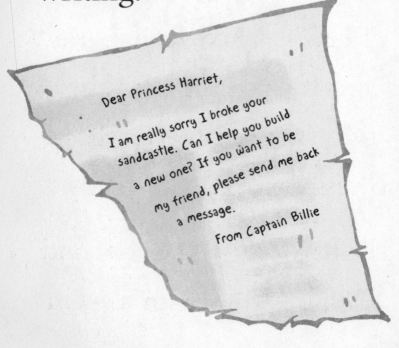

Dear Princess Harriet,

I am really sorry I broke your
sandcastle. Can I help you build
a new one? If you want to be
my friend, please send me back
a message.

From Captain Billie

Billie rolls the message up tightly and puts it inside one half of the bottle. She puts the other half of the bottle on top. Then she takes a hair-tie and wraps it around the two halves. It holds the message inside perfectly.

Billie waits for Harriet and Charlotte to go for a swim.

She runs over and puts the bottle on Harriet's towel. Then she runs back.

Harriet gets out of the water first. She picks up her towel. Billie sees the little green bottle drop onto the sand. Harriet picks it up.

Billie holds her breath and looks away. She can't bear to watch!

Then Charlotte runs
towards Billie with
the bottle in her hand.
Billie opens
the bottle.
Her heart is
jumping up
and down.

But...oh dear!
The bottle is empty!
Billie hangs her head.

Harriet doesn't want to be her friend after all!

'Oh,' says Charlotte. 'I forgot. Princess Harriet said she'd love to be your friend. She also said sorry that there's no message, but she didn't have a pen and paper.'

Billie bursts out laughing.

It's not the worst day ever, it's the best day ever! Billie is on the beach, the sun is shining and, best of all, she has a brand-new friend!

Billie B Brown

Collect them all!

The Bad Butterfly
By Sally Rippin

The Soccer Star
By Sally Rippin

The Second-best Friend
By Sally Rippin

The Midnight Feast
By Sally Rippin

The Beautiful Haircut
By Sally Rippin

The Extra-special Helper
By Sally Rippin

The Perfect Present
By Sally Rippin

Play cool games and leave a message for Billie at
www.BillieBBrown.com